What's UP, Bear?

Owlkids Books Inc.
10 Lower Spadina Avenue, Suite 400, Toronto, Ontario M5V 2Z2
www.owlkidsbooks.com

Distributed in Canada by University of Toronto Press
5201 Dufferin Street, Toronto, Ontario M3H 5T8

Distributed in the United States by Publishers Group West
1700 Fourth Street, Berkeley, California 94710

Library and Archives Canada Cataloguing in Publication

Wishinsky, Frieda
    What's up, Bear? : a book about opposites / written by Frieda
Wishinsky ; illustrated by Sean L. Moore.

Issued also in electronic format.
ISBN 978-1-926973-41-8

    1. Polarity--Juvenile literature. 2. English language--Synonyms
and antonyms--Juvenile literature. 3. New York (N.Y.)--Description
and travel--Juvenile literature. I. Moore, Sean, 1976- II. Title.

PE1591.W57 2012   j428.1   C2011-907773-6

Library of Congress Control Number: 2011943508

Design: Barb Kelly

Canadian Heritage · Patrimoine canadien

Canada Council for the Arts · Conseil des Arts du Canada

Canada

ONTARIO ARTS COUNCIL
CONSEIL DES ARTS DE L'ONTARIO

Ontario
Ontario Media Development Corporation
Société de développement de l'industrie des médias de l'Ontario

We acknowledge the financial support of the Canada Council for the Arts, the Ontario Arts Council, the
Government of Canada through the Canada Book Fund (CBF) and the Government of Ontario through
the Ontario Media Development Corporation's Book Initiative for our publishing activities.

Manufactured by C&C Joint Printing Co., (Guangdong) Ltd.
Manufactured in Shenzhen, China, in April 2012
Job #HM1569

A   B   C   D   E   F

Publisher of Chirp, chickaDEE and OWL
www.owlkids.com

What's UP, Bear?

A Book About Opposites

Written by Frieda Wishinsky • *Illustrated by Sean L. Moore*

Yes! We're going on a trip to New York City!
Doesn't the city look big and beautiful, Bear?

No! *It's big and scary, Sophie.*

Hurray! We're **up**, Bear.

Hurray! We're **down**, Sophie.

Isn't it fun to go **fast**?

I like **slow** better.

It's so **tall**!

We're so **short**.

Yeah! I'm dancing **over** the bridge.

Yikes! I'm hiding **under** the sweater.

Go, *train*, **go!**

Stop, *train*, **stop**.

Hello, *dinosaur!*

Goodbye, *dinosaur!*

Poor **wet** Bear.

Nice **dry** Bear.

See those **fancy** bears?

See this **plain** Bear.

Lots of **new** bears!

Just one **old** Bear.

Big bears everywhere!

Small *Bear right here.*

Oh no! We **forgot** Bear — but where?

Please, Sophie, **remember** Bear.

Bear is **lost**.

Bear is **found**!

I was **sad** without you.

I'm **happy** now.

Empire State Building

The Empire State Building is the tallest skyscraper in New York City. Completed in 1931, it soars up to 102 stories.

Brooklyn Bridge

Opened in 1883, the Brooklyn Bridge is a stately suspension bridge that runs across the East River. It connects Manhattan and Brooklyn—two boroughs in New York City.

The Subway

The New York City Subway system was built over a hundred years ago. Its trains run underground and aboveground, and many run day and night, 365 days a year.

LaGuardia Airport

LaGuardia is one of three big airports around New York City. It's on the waterfront of Flushing Bay and Bowery Bay in Queens, New York.

Times Square

Times Square, in the heart of Manhattan, is a busy place buzzing with neon lights. You can see lots of live theater nearby, and on New Year's Eve, hundreds of thousands of people gather in Times Square to celebrate.